GW00864364

This book
belongs to
....

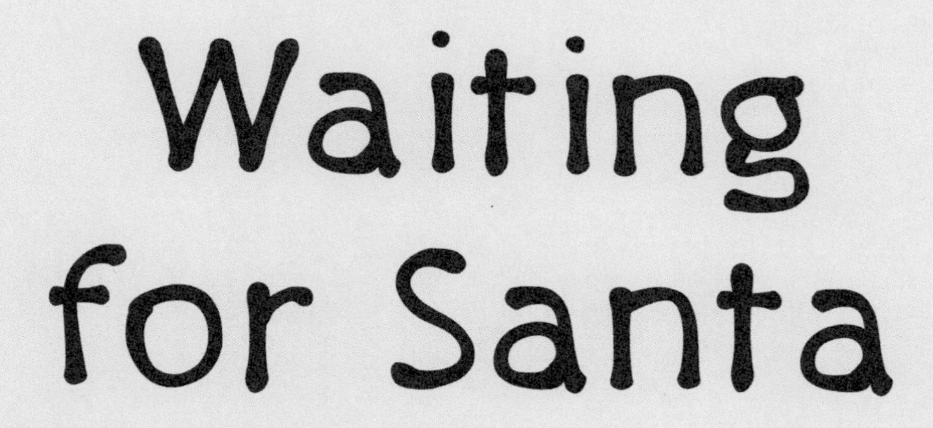

Waiting for Santa

Written and illustrated by Leila Nabih

Yawwwnnn

On Christmas Eve …

Yes?

Shall we get ready for bed?

No. I'm waiting for Santa.

Okay. Let's tidy up while we wait for Santa.

Okay.

Well done Bear! Now let's go and put our pyjamas on.

No! I'm
waiting for
Santa . . .

We can wait for Santa in our pyjamas.
But . . .

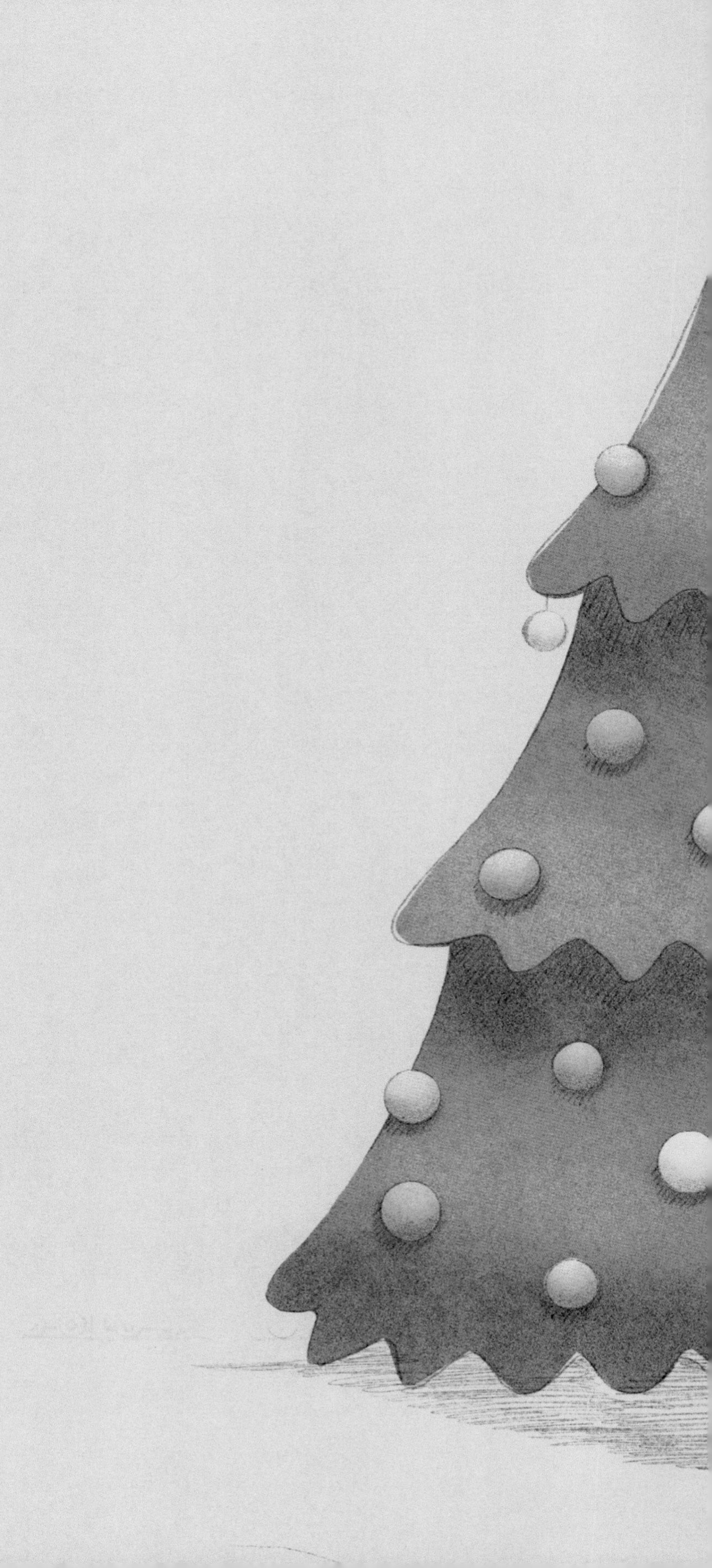

Bear reluctantly put his pyjamas on.

No ! I'm
waiting for
Santa!

It'll be quick. I promise. If I hear him coming, I'll let you know.

Well done Bear !
What would you
like to read
tonight?

BEAR
LOVES
PEARS

I love this book! Shall we get started?

NO !
I'M WAITING
FOR SANTA !

I know Bear. We can read the story while we wait for him .
No... I'm waiting for Santaaaa.....
Yaawwnn ...

BEAR
LOVES
PEARS

Zzzzzzz . . .

Creak!
Creak!
BEAR LOVES PEARS

Zzzz . . .

And a few hours later….

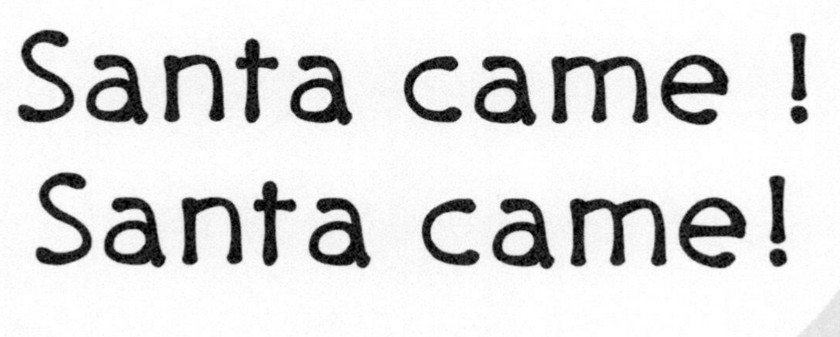
Santa came !
Santa came!

Bear
Mum

Dad

Printed in Poland
by Amazon Fulfillment
Poland Sp. z o.o., Wrocław